The Jolly Witch

by ROBERT BURCH

illustrated by Leigh Grant

E. P. Dutton & Co., Inc.   New York

JEFFERSONVILLE TOWNSHIP PUBLIC LIBRARY
JEFFERSONVILLE, INDIANA

Text copyright © 1975 by Robert Burch
Illustrations copyright © 1975 by Leigh Grant

Library of Congress Cataloging in Publication Data

Burch, Robert   The jolly witch

SUMMARY: Unappreciated by her somber fellow witches,
young, pretty, and jolly Cluny tries a new life with
some somber human beings.

[1. Witches—Fiction]   I. Grant, Leigh, ill.   II. Title.
PZ7.B91585Jr   [E]   75-5891   ISBN 0-525-32797-5

Published simultaneously in Canada by Clarke,
Irwin & Company Limited, Toronto and Vancouver

Designed by Riki Levinson
Printed in the U.S.A.
10 9 8 7 6 5 4 3 2

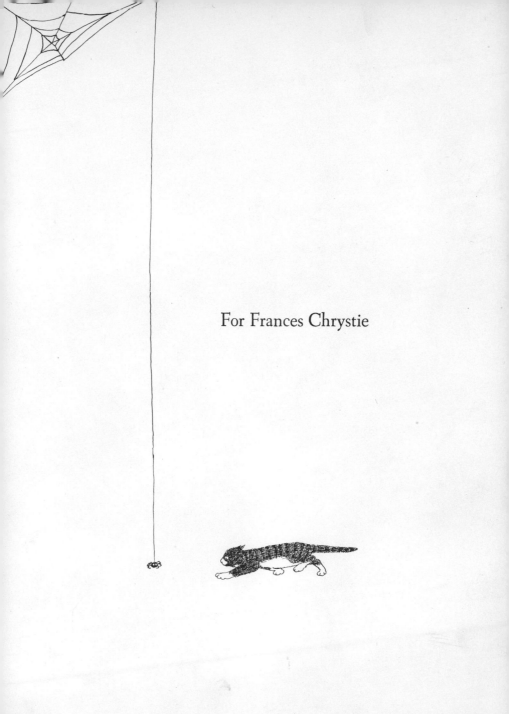

For Frances Chrystie

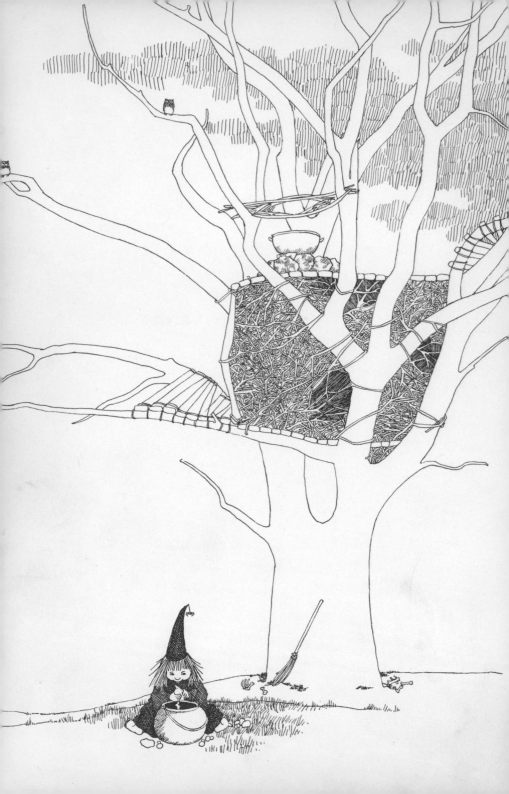

The other witches were mean to Cluny. She was young and pretty, but worst of all she was jolly. That was more than they could stand. They never let her go with them on scary trips or do anything that was fun. And the only broom they allowed her to ride was Ol' Blue, the one with a blue handle.

Redstick, the broom with a red handle, could fly upside down, and Big Yellow could do one loop-the-loop after another. Even Pinky was all right. It did not know any tricks, but it flew wherever its rider wanted to go.

Ol' Blue never wanted to go anywhere. It behaved very well on short flights, but on long ones it was apt to turn around in midair and streak back across the sky. At such times Cluny had to hang on tightly and return to the witches' den on it. Still she did not complain. After all, she was a jolly witch.

"Too jolly!" agreed the other witches, and when
they could not stand her cheerfulness another day,
they traded her off. They swapped her to a peddler
for a boxful of snakes and two iron kettles.

The head witch cackled into her ear, "Just fly back
if you ever stop being jolly!"

"Then give me a broom," whispered Cluny. With
Big Yellow she could come back doing one loop-the-
loop after another. That would be grand. Instead, Ol'
Blue was put into the crate with her, and the peddler
carted them out of the woods.

At a farm along his route, the peddler stopped at a gloomy gray cottage. Shutters hung half off their hinges, and the yard was filled with weeds. The place belonged to a cross old woman who lived there with her son, who never smiled, a brindle cat that whined constantly, and a canary that never sang. The old woman yelled to the peddler, "What are you doing out there?"

"Go look on the porch!" answered the peddler as he drove away.

"He must have brought my holly switch," the old woman said to her son.

"Holly switch?"

"To use on the cat if it should stop whining or the canary if it tries to sing—or you, if you should ever smile!" She dragged the crate into the cottage. "Holly switches are best of all, and I asked the peddler to bring me one from the deep woods. But I didn't know it would come like this!"

When the crate was opened, Cluny stepped out.
"Hello!" she said.

"Who are you?" asked the old woman.

"I'm a jolly witch."

"That stupid peddler!" cried the old woman. "A
jolly witch instead of a holly switch. He doesn't listen
to what I tell him."

"I'm glad he made a mistake," said her son.

"Oh, thank you," said the jolly witch, bowing so
low that her pointed hat began to fall off. "Let me
introduce myself. My name is Cluny."

12

"My name is Harmon," said the young man, but the old woman did not introduce herself. Instead, she pushed the young witch into the crate. "Quick!" she said to Harmon, "nail up the boards! We're sending her back."

Cluny squeezed out. "You're not making me feel welcome!"

"That's because you're *not* welcome!" said the old woman.

Cluny looked around the room. "It's a little drab
... and cold and musty ... and dusty too. Why, it's
just the way a home should be. I think I'll like it
here!" She gave the cross old woman a slap on the
back and smiled at Harmon. Then she looked at the
brindle cat and screamed, "How awful!" Quickly she
picked up the cat, ran to the door, and tossed it across
the yard. It landed at the edge of the road near the
mailbox.

"Just what do you think you're doing?" asked the old woman. "When I want the cat thrown across the yard, I'll throw it across the yard. But nobody else does. Understand?"

"But didn't you know," said Cluny, "it's bad luck to have a cat that isn't black? Goodness, there's no telling what might happen if you keep it."

"Well, the cat stays," said the old woman.

"All right," said Cluny, "if you want to risk it." She shrugged and smiled again at Harmon, but, of course, he did not smile back. It was a pity, she told herself, that anyone so handsome should look so sad.

"I want to risk it!" said the woman crossly. "And I
want to know if you're a real witch."

"Yes, but not a very good one. I was traded off because I'm too jolly."

"I'd have traded you off too," said the old woman.

"I wouldn't have," said Harmon.

"I don't seem to be getting less jolly," said Cluny.
"But if I ever do, I'll just fly back."

"Can you really fly?" asked the old woman.

"Watch me again," said Cluny, flying into the air. She did not want to give Ol' Blue time to turn and streak across the sky to the witches' den, so she circled the chimney and came back to the ground.

"Beautiful!" said Harmon.

"Thank you. It comes from practice."

"Then I'll practice," said the old woman, hopping onto her broom. She fell on her face again, but she got up and started over.

After that, she practiced on her broom from early morning until sundown. She made Cluny do the cooking, but Cluny didn't mind. In a big kettle over an open fire she prepared dishes with a spidery flavor. And, of course, she had to give the woman a flying lesson every day.

It was not long before the old woman could skim across the yard—not really flying, but not touching the ground very often.

"I can teach myself now," she told Cluny. "When the peddler comes, I'm sending you back!"

"Maybe you could teach yourself to fly low," said Cluny, "but how can you ever learn to fly high?" She added, "Like this!" and sailed into the sky on Ol' Blue.

Drifting in and out of the clouds, she thought about Harmon. She still had not seen him smile, but he was not as sad-faced as he had been. Then she felt the broom start to turn in midair. "Oh, no!" she said. She had forgotten about Ol' Blue's way of suddenly taking off to the witches' den. She pulled back on the broom.

"This time we go where the rider wants to go!" she said firmly, but Ol' Blue kept trying to turn. Cluny pulled with all her might. At last, her strength almost gone, she made the broom take her to the ground. "What a struggle!" she gasped.

"What did you say?" asked the old woman.

"I said, 'What fun it is to fly high!'"

"Get on with your work!" snapped the woman. "I'll send you away when I've learned to fly high."

Cluny was glad to start cooking. It would soon be time for lunch, and Harmon, who had been plowing all morning, would be hungry.

Just as he came over to the fire, she waved her hands over the pot, shook her head from side to side, and said strange-sounding words. She explained, "I'm flavoring the stew."

"Why not try salt and pepper," he said, "and use the stove in the kitchen?"

"If you'd like that better, I will," said Cluny, and she went out and asked the old woman how to cook on a stove.

The old woman, who was resting on the roof, leaped to the ground. "I'll show you how to use the stove if you'll teach me witch recipes."

"A new one every day!" promised Cluny.

After that, the old woman cooked over the open fire outside. She waved her hands in the air and said *abadaba-kabloom* and *hobble-itchy-gobble*.

Cluny, at the stove, began using such things as salt and pepper and tomato catsup to season her dishes. She quit using spiders altogether, although once, when there was a tiny weevil in the oatmeal, she did not fish it out.

One day when she was shelling walnuts for a pie, she threw the shells on the floor. They were scattered everywhere. "I'll sweep them away for you," said Harmon, taking a broom and sweeping out the shells.

"What a clever way to use a broom!" said Cluny, and the next day she took Ol' Blue and swept the cottage. "Now isn't this amazing?" she said. "A clean room is not at all depressing!"

The canary suddenly began to sing. Its song was a sad one. "You sound terrible," said Cluny, "but don't give up!" It started to sing again but stopped when the old woman glided past the open window. The cat, napping in the doorway, stood up and stretched.

Just then a shrill scream came from the yard.

Cluny rushed outside, and Harmon came running from the field. The old woman was at the top of a tall pine tree. Her skirt was caught on a limb, and she was dangling from it. "GET ME LOOSE!" she yelled—just as the skirt ripped and she fell to the ground.

"Are you hurt?" asked Cluny.

"Let me help you into the house," said Harmon, but the old woman sprang to her feet and began to laugh in a cackling sort of way.

"What's funny?" asked Cluny.

"You're going back to the witches," said the old woman. "I don't need you any longer because I can fly high. That's what's funny! How do you think I got to the top of the tree? I was trying to go over it, and I almost made it! Yes, indeed, you're going back!"

Cluny looked at Harmon, who looked more unhappy than ever, and started slowly toward the cottage. Then she stopped and turned to the old woman, a twinkle in her eyes. "It's lovely that you've learned to fly so well. Why, I expect you could ride *my* broom now!"

"Of course I could!" snapped the old woman. "Bring it to me and I'll show you."

Cluny ran into the cottage and brought out Ol'
Blue.

"Hang on tight!" she said to the old woman, who
grabbed the broom and took off.

She almost crashed into the barn, and when she
went over the well shelter her cap fell off her head.
But she kept flying. Then, when she had just cleared
a haystack, it happened: Ol' Blue turned around in
midair! With a SWOOSH it streaked across the sky,
and soon the old woman, hanging on with both hands,
was out of sight.

"She's gone," said Harmon.

"Forever!" said Cluny.

Harmon looked at her and smiled . . . and the cat, instead of whining, purred softly . . . and the canary, for the first time ever, sang a happy song.

31

ROBERT BURCH has written a number of fine children's books; in fact, *The Jolly Witch* is number 13, which he takes as a good omen for a witch story! Born and bred in Georgia, where he returned to live a few years ago, he has lived abroad as a civil servant, circled the globe on freighters, and spent eight years in New York City, where he first became interested in writing. He says that the reversal-of-roles idea triggered this story. He felt that in children's books "the characters usually end up being happy as whatever they were in the first place."

LEIGH GRANT has also returned to the place where she grew up, Connecticut. She is a graduate of Hollins College in Virginia and the Pratt Institute in New York. She also spent a year in Paris at the Sorbonne and then lived in London. A former art director of *Early Years* magazine, she has illustrated several children's books, including *Naomi in the Middle* by Norma Klein (Dial). She enjoyed illustrating *The Jolly Witch* because it gave her a chance to use some of the background acquired in England, as well as her interest in animals and all facets of country life.

The display type was set in Windsor Light and the text type in Fairfield. The art was prepared in pen and ink and the book was printed by offset at Halliday Lithographers.